DOLPHIN'S FIRST DAY

The Story of a Bottlenose Dolphin

SMITHSONIAN OCEANIC COLLECTION

To Robert
—K.Z.

This book is for Stephanie, Christopher,
Joseph, Daniel, Nicholas and Anthony…
for all they give to us.
—S.P.

Text copyright © 1994 by Kathleen Weidner Zoehfeld.
Book copyright © 1994 by Trudy Management Corporation,
165 Water Street, Norwalk, CT 06856, and the Smithsonian Institution, Washington, DC 20560.

Book Design: Shields & Partners, Westport, CT

10 9 8 7 6
Printed in Singapore

Acknowledgements:
   Soundprints would like to thank Dr. Charles Handley of the department of vertebrate zoology at the Smithsonian's
National Museum of Natural History for his curatorial review, and Jack Schneider, Program Director of The Maritime
Center at Norwalk (Connecticut), for providing additional support and guidance for this book.
   Steven James Petruccio would like to thank Peg Siebert, Children's Librarian at Blodgett Memorial Library, for her
research assistance and appreciation of children's books, Dana Meachen for providing the necessary
atmosphere for creativity, and Evelyne and Bud Johnson for their enthusiastic support of his work.

Library of Congress Cataloging-in-Publication Data

Zoehfeld, Kathleen Weidner.

Dolphin's first day : the story of a bottlenose dolphin / by Kathleen Weidner Zoehfeld ;
illustrated by Steven James Petruccio.
         p.   cm.
Summary: Describes a baby dolphin's experiences during his first day in the ocean.
         ISBN 1-56899-024-3
1. Dolphins — Juvenile fiction. [1. Dolphins — Fiction.]
I. Petruccio, Steven, ill. II. Title.
         PZ10.3.Z695Do 1994   93-27270
         [E] — dc20   CIP
                                                                                            AC

DOLPHIN'S FIRST DAY

The Story of a Bottlenose Dolphin

by Kathleen Weidner Zoehfeld   Illustrated by Steven James Petruccio

Soundprints

A Division of Trudy Management Corporation
Norwalk, Connecticut

Early one morning, in the wide blue sea off the coast of Florida, a baby dolphin is born.

He nestles close to his mother's side as they rise slowly through the water.

Another dolphin swims nearby. She strokes the little calf with her flipper. The dolphin is his mother's best friend. She will be his nanny.

Little Dolphin feels his mother and nanny nudging him — pushing him — up through the water — up, until he feels cool air on his back.

Pfoosh! He opens the blowhole on the top of his head and takes his first breath.

He lifts his head and peeks out above the water. In all directions, as far as he can see, the ocean sparkles like melted gold. He looks up at a vast blue sky. The sun is a golden fire on the horizon.

The morning air is quiet. But below him the ocean depths are alive with strange sounds — the little pops of snapping shrimp, the distant croaks and creaks of pilot whales, the grunts and squeaks of a thousand different fishes.

Closer by, he hears clicks and whistling noises. He sees the gliding shapes of other dolphins. Altogether, there are eight dolphins in his pod — three mothers with babies and two nannies.

The pod swims slowly, letting Little Dolphin and his mother rest after the tiring birth.

Down through the water, then up again for another breath, Little Dolphin begins to fidget. He is getting hungry. Mother rolls over and swims on her side. Little Dolphin learns to drink milk from his mother. He is sloppy at first, spilling milk everywhere.

The milk makes him feel strong and frisky. He practices pushing his flukes and flippers up and down through the water.

Soon he will be swimming like an expert.

The grownups approach Little Dolphin and gaze at him.
They make soft whistling noises. Little Dolphin tries to whistle back.
"*Chirp, chirp,*" he tries. His whistle is shaky and feeble.
  "*Peep, squeak.*" He practices his whistle again and again.

Soon Little Dolphin notices the grownups' whistling becoming louder and quicker.

They all begin to swim fast. They spread out. Now the grownups are looking for fish.

Little Dolphin feels himself being pulled along at Mother's side, the silvery water racing past his body.

Tick, tick, tick, tick, TICK, TICK, TICK. He hears the waters around him vibrate with the sound of the dolphins' echolocation signals. *TICK, TICK, TICK, TICK, TICK.*

Their clicking sounds are propelled through the water ahead of them. Before long, they hear the clicks bouncing off hundreds of small moving shapes in the water.

Echo-sense tells them a school of mullet is up ahead. They charge in closer.

Nanny takes a turn watching the baby as his mother hunts. All around Little Dolphin, mullet swim and slap the water frantically.

His mother circles a fish quickly. She flings the fish high in the air with her snout and it lands on the water with a smack. She dashes over and lifts the stunned fish in her beak.

The air above fills with the thump and swoosh of pelican wings and the squawk of hungry gulls.

The birds dive at the surface of the water and pick off the fish the dolphins leave.

Excited by the noise and smell of the hunt, a shark appears out of murky depths.

Nanny sees it. Little Dolphin feels his nanny's heart begin to pound. Nanny whistles, and Mother moves in close by her side. They make a snug cradle for Little Dolphin between them. He feels them pull him as they race down through the water — down to safety — one flipper on Mother's back, one flipper on Nanny's.

CRACK! CRACK! The older dolphins fire out sharp sound waves toward the shark. The shark turns away, confused.

For a moment, up above his head, Little Dolphin can see one of the older dolphins charging after the shark. Her skin is streaked with scars — some of them from other tangles with sharks.

THUMP! The dolphin bangs the shark sharply in the gills, and he turns and swims away.

25

Little Dolphin and his mother and nanny return to the surface.

Dolphins from another pod arrive, and some of the grownups dive down and circle around one another. They come up and slap the water with their flukes.

The dolphins leap high out of the water. Little Dolphin watches. He hears them whistle and chatter.

Two older babies swim over and offer Little Dolphin a piece of seaweed. They push it back and forth as if it were a little toy.

As the sun settles down near the horizon, the other dolphins begin to go their separate ways. Little Dolphin snuggles against his mother's side.

Above, the evening sky darkens until it matches the deep blue of the ocean. Mother whistles softly to her new baby. The waves rock them back and forth, and soon Little Dolphin is asleep.

Some of the grownups fall asleep too, but they each keep one eye open, ever alert for danger.

Tomorrow, another day begins. Little Dolphin will awaken with his mother, his nanny, and his friends at his side.

They will be there for him always, protecting him, and teaching him for each new day of growing.

About the Bottlenose Dolphin

Named for their stubby bottle-shaped beak, bottlenose dolphins live in coastal and offshore waters all around the world except in polar areas. They are intelligent animals with brains as large as humans' and a life span as long as 40 or 50 years.

Dolphins are mammals. They are warm-blooded; their body temperature stays the same, no matter what the temperature of their surroundings. Young dolphins drink milk from their mothers. Unlike fish, dolphins breathe air. They do this through a blowhole on the top of their heads.

A great deal of what scientists know of dolphins comes from observing them in captivity. Therefore, much of our understanding of group dynamics and the use of echolocation as defense is still speculative.

Glossary

blowhole: the opening of the nostrils, at the top of a dolphin's head, used for breathing.

echolocation: high-pitched clicking sounds, or ultrasounds, produced by a sound organ just inside a dolphin's blowhole. A dolphin sends these sounds forward through the water. The sounds bounce off an object and echo back to the dolphin, revealing the object's size, shape and location.

flippers: the flat paddle-like limbs on a dolphin's sides used for steering and balance while swimming.

flukes: the flattened part of a dolphin's tail, which moves up and down providing propulsion for swimming.

gills: the special organs fish use to take oxygen out of the water for breathing, usually located below and just behind each eye.

mullet: silvery fish that grow to about one foot in length and swim together in large schools.

pod: a group of dolphins that swim together.

school: a group of fish that swim together.

Points of Interest in this Book

pp. 4-5 manta ray.

pp. 16-17 With their powerful tail flukes, dolphins can swim twenty to thirty miles per hour.

pp. 20-21 brown pelicans, herring gulls.

pp. 22-23, 24-25 great white shark.

pp. 26-27 alaria (seaweed).

pp. 30-31 Dolphins only rest half of their brain at a time; they may sleep with one eye open to watch for danger.